CONTENTS

These stories first appeared in *Enid Blyton's Merry Story Book*, *Enid Blyton's Lucky Story Book* and *Enid Blyton's Happy Story Book*, all published by the Brockhampton Press.

© Text Brockhampton Press now Hodder & Stoughton Children's Books
© Illustrations Award Publications Limited 1980. Spring House,
Spring Place, London NW5 England
ISBN 0 86163 025 4
Printed in Hungary

My Best Book of Enid Blyton Stories

to DESIREE JOE
Christina JOE

Illustrated by
Rene Cloke

FROM: Auntie Heather

AWARD PUBLICATIONS

THE LOST HUM

IN the nursery cupboard there was a big humming-top. The toys loved it very much, for often when it spun round and round, and hummed loudly, it would let some of the smaller toys sit on it and hold tightly to the handle. Then they had a fine ride, as you can imagine.

But one day the humming top didn't hum! It spun round and round, but not a single hum came out of it. It was most strange.

"What has happened?" wondered the toys.

"I think it must be because Eileen sat on the top yesterday, and bent it," said the golliwog. "It must have spoilt the hum. What a pity!"

The top was sad. What was the use of being a humming-top if you couldn't hum? It sat and moped in the corner, and wouldn't even spin itself to give the small dolls and the Noah's ark animals a ride.

"We must get back your hum somehow," said the sailor doll. So one by one the toys tried to mend the hum. They pulled the handle straight. They rubbed up the silver sides. They blew in the holes—but it wasn't a bit of good. No hum came from the top at all.

"We will go to the bees and ask them if they will give us a hum for you," said the sailor doll at last. "They hum loudly, and it would be lovely if we could get a good bee-hum for you! We will go tonight!"

So that night the golliwog and the sailor doll climbed down the apple-tree that grew outside the nursery window, and went to the bee-hive. The bees were all inside, asleep. Not a hum was to be heard. The golliwog knocked on the hive.

"Zzzzzz!" said a sleepy bee at the door and he peeped out. "What do you want?"

"Could you spare a good hum for the top in the nursery?" asked the golliwog, politely.

"Zzzz! What will you give us if we do?" asked the bee.

"What do you want?" said the doll.

"There is nothing we want," said the bee. "But there's something we don't want!"

"What is that?" asked the doll, puzzled.

"Zzzzz! Well, we don't want the blue tit to come and eat us as we go in and out of our hive," said the bee. "He flies down here and waits for us. Go and tell him not to do this, and get his promise—and we will give you a good hum for the top."

So off to the blue tit's roosting-place went the golliwog and the sailor doll. They climbed up the pear-tree, where the tit slept in a cosy hole, and rapped on the bark. The tit hissed and asked what they wanted.

"Will you promise not to go and eat the bees as they come in and out of the hive?" asked the golliwog. "We want a new hum for our top in the nursery and they will give us one if you will promise not to eat them any more."

"Well, what will you give me if I promise?" asked the tit, sleepily. "I must have some food, mustn't I?"

"Well, what other food do you like?" asked the sailor doll.

"I love nuts," said the tit. "But no one has put out any nuts for me this year."

"We will go and ask the squirrel for some nuts for you," said the toys. So down they climbed and went to look for the frisky squirrel. They knew he lived in a tree-hole too—one much bigger than the tiny one the tit slept in. They soon found the oak tree that the squirrel liked, and once more up they climbed. The squirrel was sound asleep and most astonished to see them.

"Nuts!" he said. "Fancy coming and asking me for nuts at this time of night! You must be mad! What do you want them for?"

"To give to the tit," said the doll. "You see, if we take him some nuts, he says he will promise not to eat the bees, and then they will give us a hum for our big top in the nursery."

"Well, I'll find you some nuts if you like," said the squirrel, yawning, "but you must do something for me if I get up now and hunt for them."

"What would you like?" said the toys.

"I always hide my nuts in different places in the autumn," said the squirrel. "But when I wake up on a warm day, do you suppose I can remember where I have put them? No, I never can! Well, if you could get a notebook and put down in it all my hiding-places, and read them to me when I wake up on warm days, that would be such a help. If you'll do that, I'll get you the nuts you want for the tit—and what is more, I'll get the kernel out for you, because I know the tit can't, with his little beak!"

9

"Oh, thank you!" said the toys joyfully. The sailor doll put his hand into his pocket and pulled out a very small note-book and tiny pencil. He was very proud of these and had never used them before. He licked the pencil and opened the book.

"Now, I'm ready!" he said to the squirrel. "Tell me what to put down."

"There are nuts in the hole under the roots of this tree," said the squirrel, thinking. "Have you got that down? And there are some in the ditch by that old boot. And I put some more behind that thick ivy on the old wall. And the last lot I put in my own hole here. That's all."

The doll wrote down all the hiding-places in his neat, small writing. Then he shut the book and put it into his pocket. "Come to the nursery window whenever you wake up on warm winter days," he said, "and I will read you all your hiding-places. Then you will be able to eat your nuts whenever you like!"

"Thank you," said the squirrel. He groped down in his hole and brought up four fine hazel nuts. He gnawed them with his strong teeth, and made a hole in each one, so that the nut inside showed through. Then he gave the four gnawed shells to the doll.

"There you are!" he said. "The tit can peck out the nut easily now."

"Thank you," said the toys, gratefully, and went to the tit's tree. He was delighted with the nuts, and began to peck the kernel of one at once.

"Will you give us your promise not to eat the bees now?" asked the golliwog. The tit nodded his blue head.

"I promise!" he said. So off went the toys to the bee-hive and told the bees the good news. Two or three of them were waiting for the toys at the hive entrance. They were delighted to know that the tit would no longer come to eat them as they went in and out of the hive.

"Zzzzz!" they said. "Good! Now, toys, take this little pinch of yellow powder, and put it into the holes round the sides of the top. Spin the top well immediately afterwards, and you will find that it hums as loudly as a hive of bees!"

The toys thanked the bees and hurried off once more. They climbed up the apple tree and slid down to the floor. They ran to the top and emptied the fine yellow powder into all the holes. Then, amid great excitement—for all the toys had come out of the cupboard to watch—the golliwog spun the big top round and round.

"Zzzzz!" hummed the top, so loudly that the golliwog was afraid it would wake everyone up! He stopped the top in a hurry, and all the toys laughed in delight. The top had got a beautiful hum—much better than before! What fun!

Now, it would be happy again, and not lie in a corner and mope.

The squirrel hasn't been to ask where his nuts are yet—but one winter's morning, when the sun is shining brightly he'll peep in at the toys—and then the sailor doll will pull out his notebook and tell him all those hiding-places! I wish I could hear him telling the squirrel, don't you?

THE FLYING KITE

THE kite was very angry. It was a windy day, and Eric had taken it up to the hill to fly it. He hadn't very much string, so the kite couldn't fly very high. It tugged and it tugged, but Eric held it firmly.

"Let me fly higher, let me fly higher!" sang the kite. "The wind is strong, I want to go. Let me fly up, up, up!"

But Eric held on even more tightly, and that made the kite crosser still! It gave an enormous tug–and broke the string!

Ah, then it was free, and it went sailing up and up into the air, as high as could be, simply delighted. Eric was very sad. He had lost his beautiful yellow kite. He went home crying.

But the kite didn't care. "I don't belong to anyone now!" it sang. "I'm all alone! I can go where I wish! I shall fly to the moon!"

But suddenly the wind dropped—and so did the kite! It fell down, down, down to earth, and, dear me, it went splash into a small pond, frightening all the ducks and sending them off in a hurry.

"Oh!" said the kite, feeling cold and wet. "I am sinking! I want to fly! Eric, where are you? Come and save me!"

But Eric was far away. The kite got wetter and wetter. Then a dog came by and saw it in the pond. It splashed in and got hold of it. It brought it to the bank in its mouth, and bit two big holes in it. Then it left it there on the bank and ran off.

The wind dried the kite and so did the sun. It lay there, feeling very sorry for itself, with two holes in its pretty yellow canvas. Then suddenly it felt the wind lifting it again and off it went, high in the air, its tail swinging below it.

"I'm off, I'm off!" cried the kite. "Where shall I go? To the moon. Yes, to the moon."

14

But soon it dipped down again, and down and down —and oh dear, what a dreadful thing, it fell into a bonfire! The wind lifted it off again—but its tail was burnt right off and went up in smoke.

"Now I've no tail!" wept the kite. "How shall I fly without a tail?"

It lay there until night came and then the wind found it again and once more whipped it up into the air. It flew very high, even without a tail, but it kept turning upside down and round and round, for it now had no tail to steady it. It felt very giddy, and didn't like it at all.

"Why did I fly away from Eric?" thought the kite, sadly. "Better to be safe on the end of a string, than never to know what is going to happen to me!"

The wind dropped towards dawn—and down went the kite once more to earth. This time it dropped into a field where two donkeys slept. When the sun rose and lighted up the field one of the donkeys awoke and saw the big yellow kite not far off. It wondered what it could be and walked up to it. "Perhaps it is good to eat," thought the donkey. He began to nibble round the edge, and the kite was full of fear.

"Don't eat me!" it cried, but the donkey didn't hear. It went on nibbling and soon the other donkey came and nibbled too.

Goodness knows what would have happened to the kite if the farmer's little boy hadn't come running into the field then, and seen the kite. He shooed the donkeys away and picked up the kite.

"Oh!" he cried joyfully. "It's a fine yellow kite! My! Wouldn't it fly beautifully if I made it a tail and mended these holes and these ragged bits where the donkeys have nibbled!"

He took the kite home. His mother mended all the holes, and his father made a tail of string and paper. It wasn't a very good tail—but quite good enough to help the kite to fly.

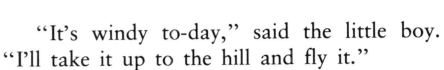

"It's windy to-day," said the little boy. "I'll take it up to the hill and fly it."

So off he went. He had the tiniest ball of string, all his mother could give him, and the kite couldn't get higher than the telegraph wires–but do you suppose it minded? Not a bit of it! It was as pleased as could be, and didn't tug at all, except just a little when the wind blew hard.

"How lovely to be held safely on a string!" thought the kite, joyfully. "What fun to fly like this! I shall never be discontented again. I will give pleasure to this little boy, instead of trying to find pleasure for myself. Then I shall be happy!"

The farmer's little boy still flies the old yellow kite and they are both as happy as can be!

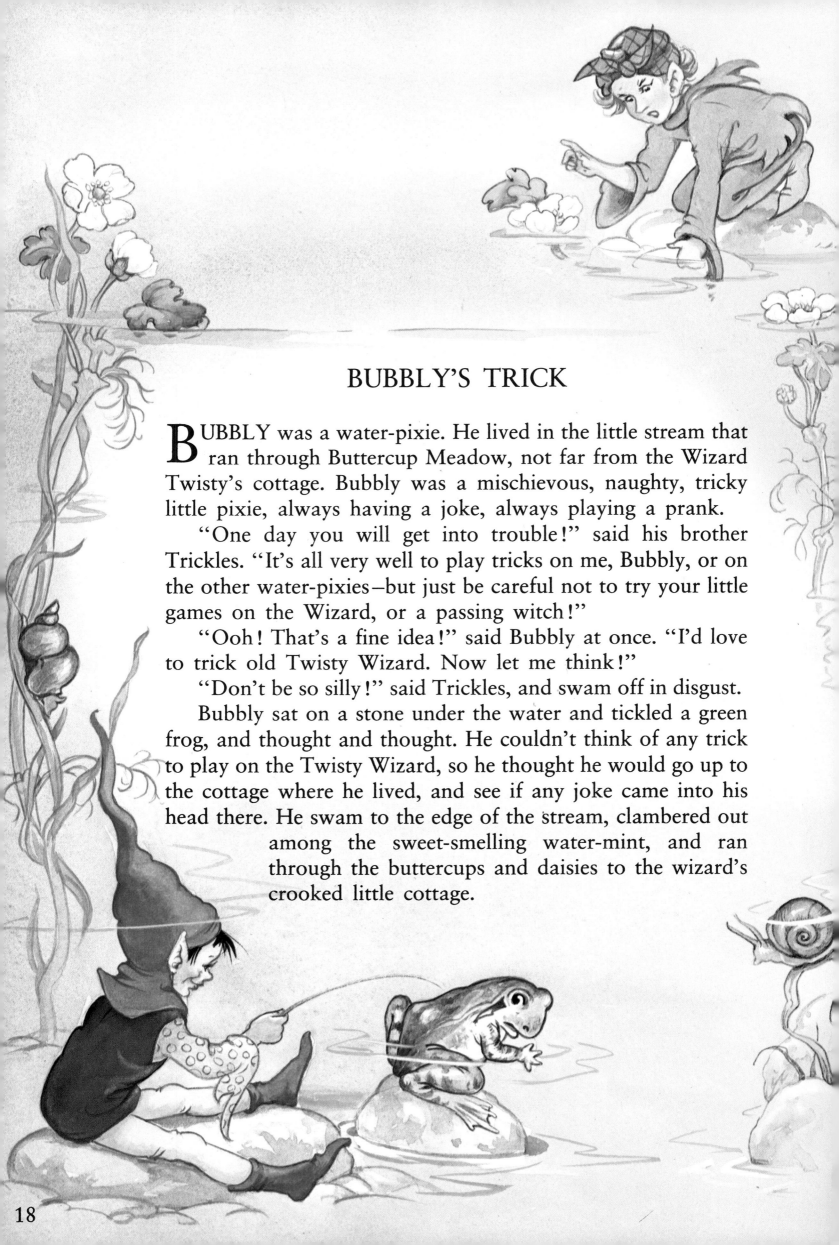

BUBBLY'S TRICK

BUBBLY was a water-pixie. He lived in the little stream that ran through Buttercup Meadow, not far from the Wizard Twisty's cottage. Bubbly was a mischievous, naughty, tricky little pixie, always having a joke, always playing a prank.

"One day you will get into trouble!" said his brother Trickles. "It's all very well to play tricks on me, Bubbly, or on the other water-pixies—but just be careful not to try your little games on the Wizard, or a passing witch!"

"Ooh! That's a fine idea!" said Bubbly at once. "I'd love to trick old Twisty Wizard. Now let me think!"

"Don't be so silly!" said Trickles, and swam off in disgust.

Bubbly sat on a stone under the water and tickled a green frog, and thought and thought. He couldn't think of any trick to play on the Twisty Wizard, so he thought he would go up to the cottage where he lived, and see if any joke came into his head there. He swam to the edge of the stream, clambered out among the sweet-smelling water-mint, and ran through the buttercups and daisies to the wizard's crooked little cottage.

He peeped in at the window. The wizard was stirring a spell in a big dish by the window. He didn't see Bubbly's cheeky face peeping in. The water-pixie chuckled and rubbed his hands. He had thought of a fine trick! He would go and buy some sherbet at the sweet-shop—and when the wizard wasn't looking he would pop it into the bowl of magic—and it would all fizzle up and give old Twisty SUCH a shock!

Off went Bubbly, and bought a pennyworth of white sherbet at the sweet-shop, in a paper bag. He stole back to the cottage and peeped in. The wizard had finished stirring his bowl of magic, and was doing something to the fire at the other end of the room. Now was Bubbly's chance!

In a trice he put his hand in at the window, shook out the powder from the paper bag, and then waited to see what would happen.

The powder fell into the bowl of magic, where strange spells were stirring. As soon as the sherbet touched the magic liquid, there came a great sizzling noise and all the stuff in the bowl rose up like a snowdrift! It frothed over the edges of the bowl on to the table, and Bubbly grinned to see such a sight.

The Twisty Wizard turned round when he heard the sizzling noise. He stared at the frothing bowl in the greatest astonishment. Then he rushed to it, shouting: "The spell has gone wrong! Jumping broomsticks, the spell has gone wrong!"

He took up the bowl and threw all the magic in it straight out of the window! And, as you know, Bubbly was just outside—so it all went over him in a trice!

He fell down in a fright, soaked through–and oh my, whatever do you think? When he got up, he had turned bright blue! He looked down at himself in horror and fear–a bright blue pixie! Whatever would everyone say to him!

"Oh, oh, oh!" wailed Bubbly, quite forgetting he was just outside the window. The wizard heard him howling, and at once popped his head out. When he saw Bubbly there, he growled like an angry dog, stretched out his hand and grabbed hold of the frightened pixie. In a moment he was standing in the kitchen before the furious wizard.

"Did you put anything into my bowl of magic?" roared Twisty.

"Yes," sobbed Bubbly. "I put some sherbet, and it made it all fizzle up."

"You wicked, mischievous, interfering, meddling creature!" cried the angry wizard. "That spell took me four months to make–and now I have thrown it out of the window!"

"It's made me all blue," sobbed Bubbly.

"Of course it has!" said Twisty. "It was a spell to make blue lightning–so it turned you blue as quick as lightning! What's your name?"

"B-B-Bubbly!" said the pixie.

"Oho! I've heard of you before!" said Twisty. "You're the pixie that makes himself a nuisance to everybody by playing stupid tricks. All right–this is the last trick you play! I shall send you to the Gobble-up Dragon to be eaten!"

Now Bubbly was indeed frightened. He tried hard to think of some way of escape. How could he outwit the wizard? He must think hard!

"Yes!" he said at last. "Send me to Gobble-up! I don't care what you do with me so long as you don't drown me!"

"Oh! So you don't mind going to Gobble-up!" said Twisty. "Well, if it's no punishment, I won't send you there. I'll pop you into my big saucepan, turn you into a goose, and have you for dinner!"

"Yes, do, do that!" said Bubbly. "But please, I do beg of you, don't drown me!"

"Oh, so you like being turned into a goose, do you," said Twisty. "Well. I'll think of something else. I'll sit you on a broomstick that will take you to the Greeneye Witch. You can be her servant for a hundred years!"

"That would be nice," said Bubbly. "Yes, do, do that, Twisty Wizard. Anything, if only you won't drown me!"

"What! You'd like to go to the Greeneye Witch," said the wizard, in surprise. "Well, I certainly won't send you there! I will turn you into a green frog and give you to my pet duck!"

23

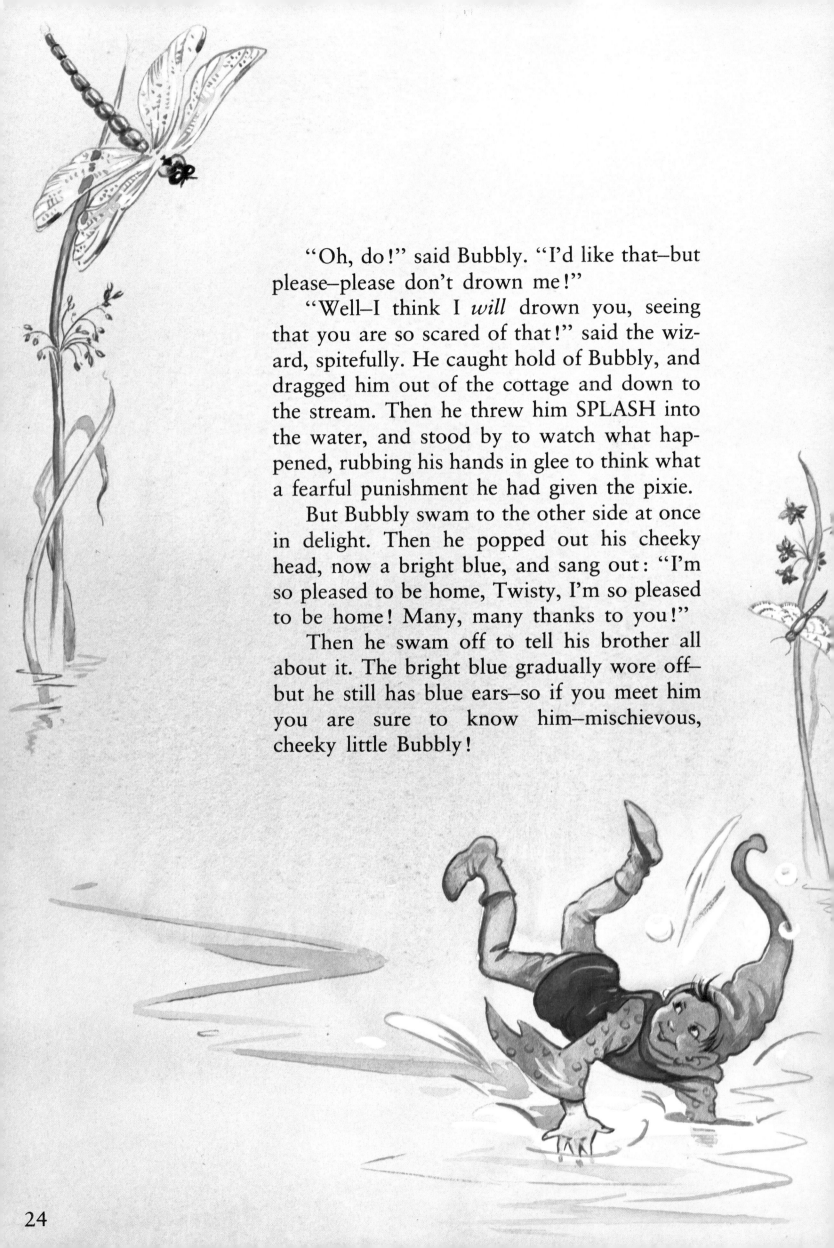

"Oh, do!" said Bubbly. "I'd like that—but please—please don't drown me!"

"Well—I think I *will* drown you, seeing that you are so scared of that!" said the wizard, spitefully. He caught hold of Bubbly, and dragged him out of the cottage and down to the stream. Then he threw him SPLASH into the water, and stood by to watch what happened, rubbing his hands in glee to think what a fearful punishment he had given the pixie.

But Bubbly swam to the other side at once in delight. Then he popped out his cheeky head, now a bright blue, and sang out: "I'm so pleased to be home, Twisty, I'm so pleased to be home! Many, many thanks to you!"

Then he swam off to tell his brother all about it. The bright blue gradually wore off—but he still has blue ears—so if you meet him you are sure to know him—mischievous, cheeky little Bubbly!

THE BLOWN-AWAY RABBIT

THERE was once a small rabbit who was a very friendly creature. His name was Bobbin, and if you could have seen his white tail bobbing up and down as he ran, you would have thought his name was a very good one!

He lived just outside the farmyard, near the pond where the big white ducks lived. He used to play with the yellow ducklings, and they were very fond of him.

One day Waggle-Tail, the smallest duck, had a terrible fright. He ran away from the others, because he wanted to see if there was a puddle he could swim on all by himself. The pond seemed so crowded when all the white ducks and the yellow ducklings were on it.

Well, Waggle-Tail waddled off to where he saw the rain-puddle shining. It was a very nice puddle indeed. Waggle-Tail sat on it and did a little swim all round it, quacking in his small duckling-voice.

The farm-cat heard him, and left his seat on the wall at once. Young fat ducklings made wonderful dinners for cats—but usually the ducklings kept with the big ducks, and the farm-cat was afraid then.

"A duckling on a puddle by itself!" said the big grey cat to himself in joy. He crept round by the wall. He crept round the pig-sty. He crouched low and waggled his body ready to jump—and just then the duckling saw him. With a terrified quack he scrambled off the puddle and ran to find his mother.

But he went the wrong way, poor little thing. He went under the field-gate instead of under the gate that led to the pond. The cat crept after him, his tail swinging from side to side.

"Quack! Quack! Quack!" cried the yellow duckling. "Quack! Quack! Quack!"

But his Mother didn't hear him. Nobody heard him—but wait! Yes—somebody *has* heard him! It is Bobbin the little rabbit!

Bobbin heard the duckling's quacking, and popped his long ears out of his burrow. He saw Waggle-Tail waddling along— and he saw the farm-cat after him.

"Waggle-Tail, Waggle-Tail, get into my burrow, quickly!" cried Bobbin. Waggle-Tail heard him and waddled to the burrow. The cat would have caught him before he got there, if Bobbin hadn't leapt out and jumped right over the cat, giving him such a fright that he stopped for just a moment.

And in that moment the little duckling was able to run into the rabbit's hole! Down the dark burrow he waddled, quacking loudly, giving all the rabbits there *such* a surprise!

Bobbin leapt into the hole too, and the friends sat side by side, wondering if the cat was still outside.

"I daren't go out, I daren't go out," quacked poor Waggle-Tail.

"I will go and fetch your big white mother-duck," said Bobbin. "I can go out to the pond by the hole that leads there. Stay here for a little while."

Bobbin ran down another hole and up a burrow that led to the bank of the pond. He popped out his furry head and called to Waggle-Tail's Mother.

"The cat nearly caught Waggle-Tail. He is down my burrow. Please will you come and fetch him."

So the big white duck waddled from the pond and went to fetch her duckling from Bobbin's burrow. She was very grateful indeed to Bobbin for saving her little Waggle-Tail.

"Maybe some day I shall be able to do you a good turn too," she said. And off she went, quacking loudly and fiercely at the farm-cat, who was now lying in the sun on the wall.

Now not long after that, Bobbin wanted to go and see Waggle-Tail—but when he put his nose out of the burrow he found that it was raining very hard indeed.

"You must not go out in that rain," said his mother. "Your nice fur will be soaked. Wait till it stops."

But it didn't stop. The rain went on and on and on. Bobbin was very cross. "I will borrow an umbrella," he thought. So he went to his Great-aunt Jemima, and was just going to ask her for an umbrella when he saw that she was fast asleep, with her paws folded in her shawl. But there was the big red-and-green umbrella standing in the corner!

Bobbin knew that no one should borrow things without asking, but he simply couldn't wait until Aunt Jemima woke up. So the little rabbit tiptoed to the corner and took the big old umbrella.

He scuttled up the burrow with it, dragging it behind him. He pulled it out of the hole and put it up. My goodness, it *was* a big one!

Bobbin held on to the big crook-handle and set off down the hillside. It was a very windy day, and the big purple clouds slid swiftly across the sky. A great gust of wind came, took hold of the umbrella—and blew it up into the sky!

And Bobbin went with it! He was such a little rabbit that the wind swept him right off his feet with the umbrella—and there he was, flying along in the sky, holding on to the umbrella!

He was dreadfully frightened. He clung to the handle with his two paws, hoping that he wouldn't fall, but feeling quite sure that he would, very soon. Poor Bobbin!

The wind swept him right over the pond. The ducklings looked up in surprise when they saw the enormous umbrella—but how they stared when they saw poor Bobbin hanging on to it too!

"It's a rabbit, it's a rabbit!" they cried. And Waggle-Tail knew which rabbit it was. "It's Bobbin, my dear friend Bobbin!" quacked Waggle-Tail. "Mother, Mother, look at Bobbin! He will fall. What can we do to save Bobbin? He saved me—we must save him!"

"But how can we?" said the mother-duck.

"Mother, can't you fly after him?" cried Waggle-Tail. "I know you don't often fly, because you prefer to swim—but couldn't you just *try* to fly after poor Bobbin?"

"I will try," said the big mother-duck. So she spread her big white wings and rose into the air. She flapped her wings and flew after the big umbrella. Bobbin was still holding on, but his paws were getting so tired that he knew he would have to fall very soon.

The mother-duck flew faster and faster on her great wings. She caught up the umbrella. She flew under the surprised rabbit and quacked to him.

"Sit on my back! Sit on my back!"

Bobbin saw her just below him. He let go the umbrella handle and fell neatly on to the duck's broad, soft back—plop! He held on to her feathers.

Down to the pond she went, carrying the frightened rabbit. What a welcome the little ducklings gave him! As for Waggle-Tail, he could hardly stop quacking!

"You did me a good turn, and now my mother has paid it back!" he quacked "Oh, I'm so glad you're safe!"

"So am I," said Bobbin. "But, oh dear, what about my Aunt Jemima's umbrella? It's gone to the clouds!" It came down again the next day, and fell into the field where Neddy the donkey lived. Neddy took the handle into his mouth and trotted to Bobbin's burrow with it.

"Here you are!" he said to Bobbin. "I heard that your Aunt Jemima was going to smack you for taking her umbrella without asking. I hope she hasn't smacked you yet."

"No, she hasn't," said Bobbin joyfully. "Oh, thank you, Neddy! What good friends I have!"

He ran down the burrow with the big umbrella, meaning to give it to his Great-aunt Jemima. But she was asleep again, with her paws folded in her shawl: so Bobbin quietly stood the umbrella in the corner and ran off to tell Waggle-Tail.

"Don't get blown away again, will you, Bobbin?" begged the duckling. And Bobbin promised that he wouldn't. He didn't want any more adventures just then!

BLACKBERRY TART

JANEY was very pleased because Ellen, who lived next door, had asked her and three other children to go on a blackberry picnic.

"Bring a big basket," said Ellen. "My mother knows a fine place for blackberries, and we are going to take tea with us. It will be great fun! We shall all bring our blackberries home, and our mothers will make us blackberry tart for our dinner next day."

"Oooh!" said Janey, who loved blackberry tart. "How lovely! I *shall* be excited this afternoon."

But before the afternoon came, poor Janey had an accident. Mother had asked her to go and fetch some butter from the dairy down the road. So down she went to get it—and poor Janey fell off the kerb on to her knees and cut them very badly.

She didn't cry till she got home. Mother was very sorry indeed. She bathed her knees and bandaged them.

"Dear me, look at the butter!" Mother said. "You fell on that too, Janey—it is a funny shape!"

That made Janey laugh—but she was soon in tears again, because Mother said she wouldn't be able to go to the blackberry picnic that afternoon.

"Darling, you can't possibly," said Mother. "You really couldn't walk all the way to the blackberry wood. Your knees are quite bad."

Well, Janey begged and begged—but it wasn't any use. Mother was right about the knees. Janey couldn't walk very well, and she would never get to the blackberry wood.

"I did so want to go to the picnic," said Janey, crying bitterly. "I did want to bring home lots of ripe blackberries for you, Mother. Now I shan't have a blackberry tart."

"I'll buy some blackberries and make a tart for you," said mother.

"They don't taste the same," sobbed Janey.

"Now don't be silly," said Mother. "You shall have a nice little picnic with Angela your doll this afternoon. You can squeeze through the hedge into the field at the bottom of the garden, and I will give you a picnic-basket all for yourself. You shall have tomato sandwiches, a piece of chocolate cake, and four sugar biscuits."

"Oh, I shall like that!" said Janey, cheering up, and she went to dress Angela in picnic clothes, so that it wouldn't matter if she got dirty.

Janey felt sad again when she saw the other children going off for their picnic. But Mother quickly packed her picnic-basket for her, and Janey set off down the garden, limping a little because her knees hurt her. She put Angela through the hole in the hedge and then squeezed through after her with the basket.

Janey felt hungry, so she decided to have her picnic straight away. She went over to the other side of the field and sat on a grassy bank there. She undid her packet of sandwiches.

They tasted lovely. So did the chocolate cake. Janey saved the four sugar biscuits till last—and it was just as she was eating these that she suddenly saw the blackberries.

Janey stared as if she couldn't believe her eyes! On the hedge not far off grew blackberry brambles—and these brambles were the largest, ripest blackberries that Janey had ever seen! They were thicker than she had ever seen too, growing in black clusters together.

Nobody came into that field except the farmer and his two horses, so nobody had seen the blackberries. There they were, waiting to be picked!

"Oh!" said Janey in delight. "Look at them! I can pick enough to fill my basket! Won't Mother be surprised! Now we shall have our blackberry tart after all!"

She got up and limped over to the brambles. She began picking as fast as she could. Some of the berries went into her mouth—and they *were* delicious! But most of them went into the basket.

When the basket was almost full and quite heavy, Janey squeezed back through the hedge and into her own garden again. She went up to the house and called Mother.

"I'm in the front garden!" cried Mother. So Janey went there—and just as she got there all the other children came running home with their baskets of blackberries.

"Hallo, Janey!" they cried. "It *was* bad luck that you couldn't come blackberrying with us! Look what we've got!"

"And look what I've got!" said Janey proudly, and she showed them her basket full of the big ripe berries.

"Good gracious!" said Ellen. "They are far better than ours! Wherever did you get them?"

"Mother let me have a picnic all to myself in the field at the back," said Janey. "And whilst I was having it, I saw these blackberries. Aren't I lucky?"

"You *are!*" said all the others. "Oh, Janey, we wish we'd been with you, instead of in the blackberry wood. Your berries are far bigger than ours."

"Well, it was a good thing I fell down after all," said Janey. "It's funny how bad things turn into good things sometimes!"

"It depends how you behave about the bad things," said Mother with a laugh. "If you'd been silly and sulky about not going on the picnic with the others, and hadn't gone off by yourself to the field, you'd never have found the lovely big blackberries. Well, I'll make you a fine tart to-morrow."

She did—a big juicy one, full of the ripe blackberries. Janey is going to eat it with cream. I wish I could have a slice too, don't you?

SALLY SIMPLE'S MATCHES

ONCE Sally Simple was very angry because she was always losing her matches. She wanted to light her candle, and the matches had gone again.

"Where are they, where are they?" cried Sally Simple, stamping all over the place. "I put them down by the candle, I know I did—and now they're gone again! Nobody has been here—I'm the only one in the house, so where, where have those matches gone?"

She found them at last on the window-ledge, and then she remembered that she had lent them to old Mr. Twiddle to light his pipe when he went by that morning. He had given them back to her and she had popped them on the window-sill instead of putting them by her candle.

"Now this won't do," said Sally sternly to herself. "Sally, you waste half your time looking for your matches. In the morning you cannot find them to light the fire. At night you cannot find them for your candle. You can never find them unless you hunt for ages all over the place. Now be sensible, Sally Simple, and think of a safe place to keep them in *always*."

When Sally Simple talked to herself like that, she always listened. She thought for a moment and then she nodded.

"I know where I'll keep the matches," she said. "I'll put them in my apron pocket, and then they will always be with me. All I need to do is to slip my hand into my pocket and there the matches are!"

So she put the box there, and felt very pleased with herself. She felt so pleased that she hummed all day long as she worked. Then Dame Fanny came in to see her, and told her all the news. She stayed for a cup of tea, and after she went, Sally cleared away and washed up.

It began to get dark. Sally thought she would light the lamp. She went to the lamp table and felt about for the matches, which she sometimes put there. She had quite forgotten where she had put them.

They were not there. Sally was cross. "Maybe I left them by the stove," she said. But they were not there. Then she went to the candlesticks, but there were no matches there either.

"Bother, bother, bother!" said Sally. "Now I must really go and borrow some, for I cannot see to hunt all over the place for the matches."

So she went to Mother Grumps, her next-door neighbour. She knocked at the door. "Please, could you lend me some matches?" she asked.

"I haven't any," said Mother Grumps. "Just used the last one to light my candle with. Sorry."

39

So then Sally went to the house on the other side of her cottage and knocked on the door. Mr. Tweaky lived there. He opened the door, and was pleased to see Sally.

"Come in, come in," he said. Sally stepped inside. "And what can I do for you?" asked Mr. Tweaky.

"Well, I've come to borrow a box of matches, please," said Sally. "I can't find mine, and I must light my lamp."

"There's my box over there," said, Mr. Tweaky. "Just by you–look, Sally."

Sally picked up the box–but alas it was empty! "Oh, dear–you must have used the last one. Mr. Tweaky," said Sally. "Haven't you any more?"

"Yes, I've some in my store-cupboard upstairs," said Mr. Tweaky. "Bring the candlestick, Sally, and we'll look."

Sally took the lighted candlestick and went upstairs with Mr. Tweaky. He opened the door of his big store-cupboard, but just as he did so the wind from the open window blew out he candle. They were in darkness.

"Oh dear!" said Sally. "The candle's gone out."

"Never mind," said Tweaky. "I think I know where the matches are. I'll get a chair because I think they are on the top shelf."

So he got a chair and stood on it. He felt along the top shelf, and tried to find the packet of matches. But he couldn't find them. So he stood on tiptoe and tried to reach to the very back of the shelf—and over went the chair and down went poor Mr. Tweaky with a dreadful bump!

"Oh! Oh! I've hurt myself!" he cried. "Bring a light, bring a light! I've hurt myself! Light the candle, and let me see what I've done!"

Sally Simple was dreadfully upset. She set the candlestick on the floor, and felt in her apron pocket for the matches. She struck one and lighted the candle. Then she looked at Mr. Tweaky.

He had bruised his leg and his arm very badly. Sally helped him downstairs and put him on the couch. She bathed the bruises and put bandages on—and all the time Mr. Tweaky glared at her and seemed very angry indeed.

Sally couldn't understand it. "Please Mr. Tweaky, why are you so cross?" she asked. "It was not my fault that you fell off the chair, and I have been as kind as possible to you since you did."

"I think you are a very bad person," said Mr. Tweaky. Sally began to cry.

"Why?" she asked. "I haven't done anything wrong."

"Sally Simple, you came here to ask for a box of matches—you made me go upstairs to the store-cupboard, you made me stand on a chair in the dark and feel for my matches—and when I fell down and hurt myself, what did you do?"

"I lighted your candle to see what had happened to you," sobbed Sally.

"Yes," said Mr. Tweaky : "you *took a box of matches out of your pocket,* Sally, and struck a match—after you had come to borrow *my* matches, and made me have this horrid accident. How dare you come to borrow matches when you've got some in your pocket!"

"Oh dear, oh dear, how foolish I am!" sobbed Sally. "I'd forgotten where I'd put them till that very minute, really I had, Mr. Tweaky."

"Please go home," said Mr. Tweaky. "I don't want puddles of tears all over my carpet. I'm very offended with you, Sally Simple."

So Sally went home. And will you believe it, when she put her hand into her apron pocket to get the matches to light her own lamp, they weren't there! She had left them at Mr. Tweaky's. Well, well, well! So Sally had to go to bed in the dark that night, because she really didn't dare to go and ask Mr. Tweaky for them.

Now she ties them to her candlestick every day and they can't disappear. Poor Sally!

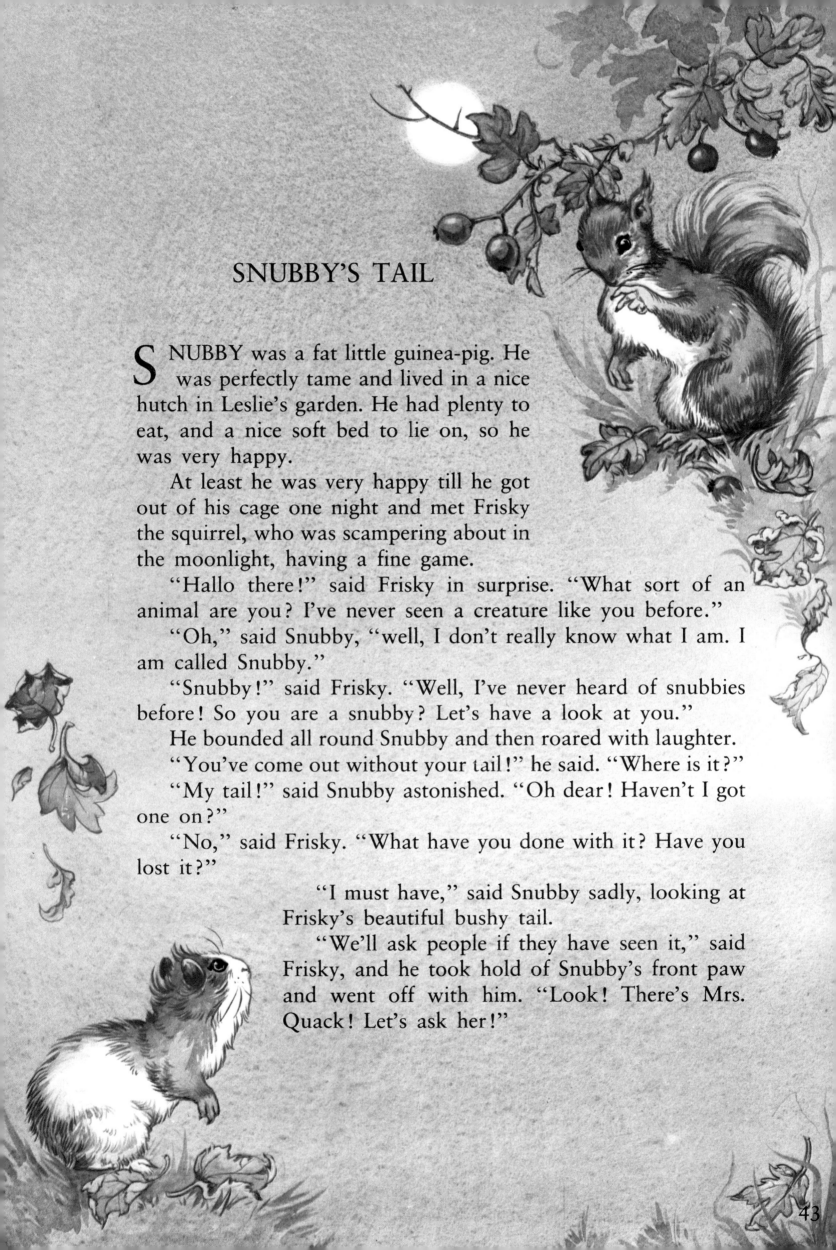

SNUBBY'S TAIL

SNUBBY was a fat little guinea-pig. He was perfectly tame and lived in a nice hutch in Leslie's garden. He had plenty to eat, and a nice soft bed to lie on, so he was very happy.

At least he was very happy till he got out of his cage one night and met Frisky the squirrel, who was scampering about in the moonlight, having a fine game.

"Hallo there!" said Frisky in surprise. "What sort of an animal are you? I've never seen a creature like you before."

"Oh," said Snubby, "well, I don't really know what I am. I am called Snubby."

"Snubby!" said Frisky. "Well, I've never heard of snubbies before! So you are a snubby? Let's have a look at you."

He bounded all round Snubby and then roared with laughter.

"You've come out without your tail!" he said. "Where is it?"

"My tail!" said Snubby astonished. "Oh dear! Haven't I got one on?"

"No," said Frisky. "What have you done with it? Have you lost it?"

"I must have," said Snubby sadly, looking at Frisky's beautiful bushy tail.

"We'll ask people if they have seen it," said Frisky, and he took hold of Snubby's front paw and went off with him. "Look! There's Mrs. Quack! Let's ask her!"

43

They went up to a large white duck who was busy diving for food in a nearby pond. She stared at Snubby in surprise when she saw him, for she had never seen such a creature before.

"This is a snubby," said Frisky. "He has lost his tail. Look!"

Mrs. Quack looked. "Dear, dear!" she said. "So he has. What a pity!" She wagged her own feathery tail to make sure she had it, and Snubby did wish he had one like hers.

"I haven't seen the snubby's tail," she said. "But Willie the dog is somewhere about, hunting rats. He may have seen it.

So Snubby, Frisky and Mrs. Quack went off together to look for Willie the dog.

He was hunting rats, and had his head down a hole. He had a fine long tail that wagged when the others spoke to him. Snubby did wish he had a tail like that.

"Hallo, hallo!" said Willie, pulling his head out of the hole and looking at the others. "What's all this? Whatever is this curious creature?"

"It's a snubby," said Mrs. Quack and Frisky together. "Isn't he curious! He hasn't a tail—look! He must have lost it. We wondered if you had seen it."

"No, I haven't," said Willie. "But there's an old rat-tail he can have if he likes."

"No, thank you!" said Snubby at once. "I'm not going to have a tail like that! I want one like Frisky's—or like Mrs. Quack's, or yours, Willie!"

"Oh, well!" said Willie, "if you're going to be so particular, I'm afraid I can't help you! I haven't seen your lost tail!"

"Don't be cross, Willie," said Frisky. "You are a clever dog—just think hard for a minute and see if you can think of some way to get back the snubby's tail!"

So Willie thought hard. Then he wuffed and said : "Of course! There's the wishing-well! If we can get old Mother Turnabout to come with us to the well, she can get Snubby's tail for us!"

So off they all went to Mother Turnabout.

She was knitting by the fire, and was most astonished to see Snubby, Frisky, Mrs. Quack and Willie walking in at the door.

"Bless us all!" she cried. "What's this? Now what have you come for at this time of night?"

"Please, Mother Turnabout, will you come with us to the wishing-well, and wish back the little snubby's lost tail for us?" begged Frisky. "He lost it coming along to-night, and he is so miserable without it."

"I've never heard of a snubby before," said Mother Turnabout, peering at Snubby through her spectacles. "Funny little
chap, he looks! Well, I'll come—but mind you, creatures—I
shall want an egg from you, Mrs. Quack—a score of nuts from
you, Frisky—and you'll please to guard my house for me for a
week, Willie. As for you, little snubby thing, I don't know if
you lay eggs or what you do—but when you've got your tail
back, you can repay me in some way!"

They all went out of the door and made their way to the
old wishing-well in Mother Turnabout's garden. She took a
shiny green stone, and dropped it down the well. Then she
spoke softly.

"Well, wishing-well, are you listening? Bring back the tail of the little snubby!"

She let down a bucket into the water, and then slowly pulled it up again. She put her hand into the bucket to get out the tail she expected to find there.

"How very strange!" she said at last. "There is no tail here! This the first time that the wishing-well has ever failed to grant a wish! I must let the bucket down again!"

Down it went again—and up it came again—but there was no tail there! Mother Turnabout grunted, and walked back to her cottage, sad and puzzled.

All the creatures followed her, quite frightened. The old dame sat down in a chair and frowned.

"I can't make it out!" she said. "Why didn't it grant my wish? Surely, oh surely, the magic hasn't gone out of my wishing-well!"

She stood up and went to the door. She called loudly: "Cinders, Cinders, Cinders!"

A big black cat with green eyes came bounding up. He was astonished to see Mother Turnabout's visitors, and he spat rudely at the dog.

"Cinders!" said the old dame. "I wished for the tail of this little snubby to come back, for he lost it this evening–and it didn't come back!"

"Then he didn't lose it," said the cat.

"But he must have!" cried Mrs. Quack, Willie and Frisky. "He hasn't got it on!"

"Let me see," said the cat. So Snubby came forward and then turned himself slowly round backwards. Sure enough, he had no tail.

But Cinders looked at him closely–and then he began to laugh, showing all his sharp white teeth.

"What's the matter?" cried everyone.

"Why, that's a guinea-pig and they don't have tails!" said the cat. "He didn't lose his tail—he never had one! Ho, ho, ho! What a joke!"

"You said he was a snubby!" cried Mother Turnabout angrily, to Frisky.

"He said he was!" cried Frisky.

"I didn't! I said my name was Snubby, and so it is!" cried Snubby quite frightened. All the animals looked so fierce that he made up his mind to run—and out of the door he went as fast as his four little legs could carry him.

"After him!" cried Willie—and out they all went, leaving Mother Turnabout in her chair, feeling very glad indeed to think that the magic hadn't gone out of her well after all!

Snubby hid under a bush and Mrs. Quack, Willie and Frisky ran by. Then out he crept and ran back to his hutch as fast as he could. How glad he was to be there once more! He shut the door with his own snubby nose and was pleased to hear the click that told him it was latched. He was safe!

"I don't want a stupid tail!" he thought. "If you have a tail, you have to keep a wag in it, and that would be such a nuisance. I'm lucky to have no tail!"

And he went to sleep, and dreamed that Mother Turnabout had stolen Frisky's tail, and Willie's tail and Mrs. Quack's as well, and had put them all into her best Sunday hat. How he laughed when he woke up! Funny little Snubby!

SUSIE AND HER SHADOW

ONCE a very funny thing happened to Susie. She was sitting in the sunshine, reading a book, when she saw a small pixie running by her with a big pair of scissors.

Susie was so surprised to see a pixie that at first she couldn't say a word. She just stared and stared. The pixie spoke first.

"Hallo!" he said. "I suppose you don't really want your shadow, do you?"

"Whatever do you mean?" cried Susie.

"Well," said the pixie, "I'm just asking you if you want your shadow. It's no use to you. It would be *very* useful to me, if you'd let me have it."

"But what do you want a shadow for?" asked Susie.

"Well," said the pixie, whispering, "you see, it's like this. I know a spell to make a magic cloak. If anyone puts on this magic cloak they will not be seen—they will be quite invisible. And I *do* want a magic cloak!"

"But what's a shadow got to do with a magic cloak?" asked Susie in surprise.

"You *are* stupid," said the pixie impatiently. "The magic cloak is made of somebody's shadow, of course. That is why I want your shadow."

"But I want my shadow too," said Susie.

"Now don't be silly and selfish," said the pixie, opening and shutting his big scissors. "What use is your shadow to you? Does it play with you?"

"No," said Susie.

"Does it help you to do your lessons?" said the pixie.

"No," said Susie.

"Does it keep you warm?" said the pixie.

"Of course not," said Susie.

"Well, then!" cried the pixie. "What's the use of it? None at all! You might just as well let me have it."

"Why don't you cut your *own* shadow?" said Susie suddenly. "If my shadow is no use to me, then yours is certainly no use to *you!* You CAN'T have my shadow, Pixie, so now you know."

Then the pixie fell into a tremendous rage and stamped about and shouted. Susie was a bit afraid at first, and then he looked so funny that she couldn't help laughing.

"Oh! So you're laughing at me, are you?" cried the little fellow in a rage. "Then I'll steal your shadow without waiting for you to say yes!"

And with that he opened his big scissors and began to cut all round poor Susie's shadow. Of course it didn't hurt her, but it was dreadful to see her pretty purple shadow being cut away behind her. She tried to stop the little pixie, but he was too quick. With three or four snips of his sharp scissors he had cut off the whole of Susie's shadow.

Then he neatly rolled it up, put it over his shoulder, laughed loudly and ran off. Susie ran after him. The pixie ran to a rabbit-burrow and disappeared down it. He was gone.

Susie began to cry. She looked behind her. She had no shadow at all, not even the tiniest one, and it was strange to be without her shadow.

"I don't feel right without my shadow," she wept. "And how every one will laugh at me. They'll call me 'The Girl Without a Shadow'!"

She was so busy crying and wiping her eyes that she did not see a fat little brownie looking at her from his house in a tree. He had opened his door, which was cut in the trunk, and was looking very puzzled.

"Little girl! Whatever's the matter?" he called at last. "You are making such a noise that I can't hear my wireless."

Susie had already had so many surprises that she hardly felt astonished at all to see a brownie looking out of a tree-house at her. She wiped her eyes and answered him.

"Well, *you'd* cry too, if you'd just had your shadow cut off by a mean little pixie who wanted to make a magic cloak with it!" said the little girl.

"Good gracious!" said the brownie, stepping out of his tree and looking closely at Susie. "You are quite right. You haven't a shadow. Well, well, well!"

"It isn't well at all," said Susie. "It isn't well at all," said Susie. "It's perfectly horrid. I simply don't know what to do. The pixie went down this rabbit-hole, and I'm too big to follow him."

"I can help you," said the brownie. "Come inside my tree-house and you can go down to my cellars. They lead into the passage to the pixie's home, just near that rabbit-burrow."

"Oh, thank you", said Susie. She climbed into the tree-house after the brownie. She had hardly time to see what it was like, because the brownie took her so quickly down some winding steps right to his cellars. He opened a door there, and Susie peered out into a dark passage.

"Where do we go from here?" she whispered.

"Follow me," said the brownie. He led the way down the passage till they came to a door marked "Mister Pixie Podge."

"This is where he lives," said the brownie. He hit the door with his fist and it flew open. Susie stared inside.

"There you are!" he said. "That's done."   Then he suddenly began to laugh. He laughed and laughed, and Susie got quite cross with him.

"Whatever's the matter?" she said.

"Well," said the brownie, giggling, "well, little girl, just look. You've got a pixie's shadow instead of your own. See the pointed ears! Oh, it's very funny!"

Susie looked round at her shadow. The brownie was perfectly right. She had a pixie shadow! Although she was a little girl, her shadow was that of a fairy. Susie suddenly felt very pleased.

"I'm glad," she said. "I'm glad. I know this isn't a dream now, because I've only got to look at my shadow and see a fairy's shadow, and I'll know it's all true! Oh, what fun!"

And off she skipped home, her pixie shadow following her and skipping too. I think she's lucky, don't you? Do you know a Susie? Well, have a look at her shadow next time you see her, and if it's like a pixie's, you'll know she's the same Susie as the one in this story!

HA, HA,
JACK-IN-THE-BOX!

OF all the toys in the nursery the great-est nuisance was the Jack-in-the-box! He was for ever jumping out of his box just when nobody was expecting him, and this was most upsetting, especially to timid creatures like the pink rabbit and the baby doll.

But the Jack-in-the-box simply loved to scare people. He thought it was great fun. He was an ugly creature, with a big red face, two little arms, and a big pink body made of a long spring. When his lid sprang open and he jumped out, he shook and jerked on his spring in a most peculiar manner. Nobody liked him.

His box was shut by a little catch. By slipping out his arm the Jack could undo his catch whenever he wanted to—then his lid would fly up and he would spring out to his full length, jerking and bouncing about in a most terrifying manner! It was a pity he could undo his own box.

One day he waited in a dark corner for the baby doll to come by, and when she trotted past, click! went his lid, and out he jumped with a yell. The baby doll fell down in fright and turned blue in the face. This made her look very strange, and it took the toys all night to get her face the right colour again. The Jack-in-the-box looked on and made rude re-marks all the time.

"One day you'll go too far," said the teddy bear angrily. "Why don't you frighten people your own size? Me, for instance!"

"All right!" said the Jack-in-the-box. "I'll give you a real scare, teddy!"

"Pooh, *I'm* not afraid of you!" said the teddy, and he gave the Jack-in-the-box a smack on his red, grinning

face. The Jack was angry and jumped after the teddy bear all over the nursery floor, making a great noise each time his box came down bang on the floor.

After that he lay in wait for the bear. He saw one night that Mollie, the little girl to whom all the toys belonged, had left a bowl of soapy water on the floor. She had been blowing big bubbles. The Jack-in-the-box placed himself just nearby and waited for the bear to come by. Soon, along he came, whistling a little tune.

"Bo!" The Jack sprang right out of his box, and gave the bear such a terrible scare that he fell right into the bowl of soapy water—which was just what the Jack meant him to do.

The Jack-in-the-box laughed so much at the sight of the bear swimming about in the water, that big tears ran all down his pink body.

"You horrid creature!" said the bear, climbing out. "I hope your tears rust your springs!"

He had to stand by the fire all night long to dry himself—and even when morning came he was a bit damp. So he got a dreadful cold and sneezed twenty times without stopping, which was very tiring.

The next night the Jack jumped out at the pink rabbit and frightened him so much that he tried to get down a crack in the floor boards and stuck half-way. It was very difficult to get him out, but the toys managed to at last.

"We won't have anything to do with that horrid Jack-in-the-box," said the toys to one another. "We won't speak to him. We won't answer him. We won't look at him. We won't ask him to any parties!"

"And we'll have a perfectly wonderful party very very soon!" said the golliwog. "Then when the Jack-in-the-box sees that he isn't even asked, he will be sorry for his bad ways!"

So a wonderful party was arranged for Friday night. There were to be chocolate buns and toffee to eat, cooked on the toy stove by the pink rabbit, who was a very good cook indeed. There was to be lemonade drunk out of the cups belonging to the doll's teaset. There were to be games of all kinds and dancing to the music of the musical box. The golliwog said they could all take turns at turning the handle round.

Everyone was asked except the Jack-in-the-box. He was furious.

"What! You're not going to ask *me!*" he cried in a rage. "Very well, then—I'll come to your party *without* being asked—and I'll jump all over the place and upset the lemonade and squash the chocolate buns—so there! Not ask me, indeed! Whatever next!"

The toys stared at one another in dismay. They hadn't thought of that. Now what were they to do?

The teddy bear beckoned to the golliwog. They went into a corner and whispered.

"I've a plan," said the bear. "If only I'm brave enough to carry it out!"

"What is it?" asked the golliwog.

"Well, what about nailing down the Jack's lid?" asked the bear. "I know where the hammer and nails are kept—in Mollie's little carpentry set. When the Jack is asleep I could take a nail, creep up to his box and nail down his lid!"

"That's a splendid idea–if only you are brave enough!" said the golliwog.

The teddy bear didn't feel brave enough until early on Friday night, an hour before the party was to begin. The golly told him that the Jack was asleep, because he had heard him snoring. The bear ran to the tool-box and took out a hammer

and a big nail. Then he crept bravely up to the Jack-in-the-box. Bang, bang! He drove the nail through the lid into the edge of the box!

The Jack woke up. He slipped out his arm and undid his catch–but what was this! His lid did not spring open as it usually did! He could not get out! He began to jerk about in his box in a rage, and the box jiggled and jolted.

"Now let the party begin!" cried the big doll. "The rabbit has made the buns and the toffee and I have poured out the lemonade in the cups!"

"Let me out, let me out!" shouted the Jack angrily. But nobody did. The party went on merrily. All the buns and the toffee were eaten, and there was no more lemonade left. The golly turned the handle of the musical box and the toys began to dance. What fun!

The Jack was taken no notice of at all. He tried his best to get out but the nail was much too strong. He had to stay shut in his box whilst the toys had a fine time.

The next day Mollie had a friend to tea, and the little boy picked up the Jack-in-the-box and tried to open the box.

"How funny, Mollie! It's nailed up!" he said. "Why did you do that?"   "I didn't," said Mollie, in surprise. "Let me look."

"Well," she said. "I don't know who nailed him up–but I think it's a good idea! I never did like him! He can stay nailed up!"

And for all I know the Jack is still tightly fastened in his box–but I dare say if he gives his solemn promise to the golliwog to behave himself in future, the toys will forgive him and take out the nail.

It was a good punishment for him, wasn't it?

THE SQUIRREL AND THE PIXIE

THERE was once a pixie called Goldie because of her shining yellow hair. All the summer she played with the swallows in the air, and when they flew away in October she was sad.

"The cold days are coming," twittered the swallows to her. "We must go. You cannot come with us, Goldie, because your wings could not fly so far. Why do you not sleep through the cold days as many of the other creatures do?"

"I think I will," said Goldie. So she set about making herself some warm rugs and blankets, a warm dress and a warm cloak.

"Then I shall be able to sleep in comfort," she told a spider who was watching her. "I shall roll myself up in all these warm clothes and sleep until the spring, just as you do, Spider."

She made her blankets of rose-petals, sewn neatly together. She made her rugs of the thistledown that she gathered from the thistles—it looked like a furry cover when she had finished it. She sewed herself a dress and a coat of crimson creeper leaves, and she did look nice in them.

Then she went to find a place to sleep in. She chose a nice cosy corner at the bottom of some big Michaelmas daisies. They waved their pretty daisy-heads far above her. She smiled at them.

"You will shelter me when it rains," she said. Then she curled herself up in her new rugs and went to sleep.

But alas for poor Goldie! In a few days' time the gardener came along and cut down all the Michaelmas daisies! They were fading, and he wanted to make the garden tidy.

He very nearly trod on Goldie. She woke up in a great fright and flew away, leaving behind her beautiful warm rugs and blankets. She saw them all put into the gardener's barrow and wheeled away to be burnt on the bonfire. She was very unhappy.

"I am so cold," she shivered. "I shall not be able to make any more covers. I shall freeze to death at night!"

A small red squirrel bounded over to her. "Why are you crying?" he asked. Goldie told him.

"Well, why don't you go and cuddle up to one of the little animals who sleep the winter days away?" he asked her. "They usually have plenty of moss and dead leaves for blankets, or at any rate some sort of shelter from winter storms."

"That's a very good idea," said Goldie, cheering up. "But where shall I find anybody? I don't know where to look."

"Oh, I'll soon show you one or two," said the squirrel. "First of all, come and see the nice cosy hole that the hedgehog is sleeping in. He always makes himself very comfortable for the winter."

Goldie took the squirrel's paw and he led her to a little hole in a dry bank. He pushed aside a mossy curtain and Goldie slipped inside. She saw a big, brown prickly hedgehog there, fast asleep, curled up warmly on some dead leaves.

She came out of the hole again and shook her head. "No, dear Squirrel," she said. "I don't want to sleep with the hedgehog. He is so prickly that I couldn't cuddle up to him —and besides, he snores! Take me somewhere else."

"Well, I'll take you to the toad," said the squirrel. "He always chooses a good, sheltered place."

So he took the pixie to a big mossy stone, and told her to creep underneath it. There she found the old toad sleeping soundly, quite safe and cosy under the stone. But Goldie crept out again, shivering.

"He has no blankets to cover himself," she said. "And it is damp under there. I wouldn't like to sleep there."

"Well, come where the bats live," said the squirrel. "They sleep very soundly indeed." So he took her to an old cave and showed her the black bats hanging upside down around the cave. But Goldie screwed up her little nose and ran outside the cave.

"They smell," she said. "I couldn't possibly sleep with the bats."

The squirrel thought for a moment. "You might like to cuddle in a heap with the snakes," he said. "They have chosen a good hollow tree this winter, and they are as warm as toast there. Come along, I'll show you."

But when Goldie peeped inside the hollow tree and saw the snakes all twisted up together, she shook her head at once.

"No," she said. "I wouldn't dare to sleep with the snakes! See how they have twisted themselves together, Squirrel! They might squeeze me to bits if they twisted round me too! No! Show me some one else, please."

"You are very hard to please, Goldie," said the squirrel, thinking hard. "There's the dormouse—he has quite a nice winter nest in the roots of the old fir tree. Would you like to go there?"

"Oh, I don't think so," said Goldie. "It sounds too stuffy to me. What about *you*, Squirrel? Where do *you* sleep?"

"Oh, I sleep in a hole in a tree, and am very cosy," said the squirrel. "But I don't sleep all the winter through, you know. I wake up when we get warm days and I go out and have a play. I eat a few of my nuts too. I hide them away so that I can have a feast in the warm winter days—we do get quite nice sunny days sometimes, you know, and I always think it's such a pity to sleep through those."

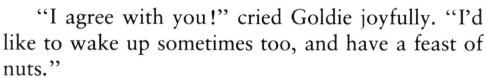

"I agree with you!" cried Goldie joyfully. "I'd like to wake up sometimes too, and have a feast of nuts."

"The only thing is—I often forget where I hide my nuts," said the squirrel. "I'd love to have you share my sleeping-hole, Goldie, if you'd help me to hunt for my nuts when we wake."

"I'll help you, I'll help you!" cried Goldie. "Now, show me where you sleep, Squirrel."

So he showed her his warm, sheltered hole in the oak tree, and together they curled up there, warm and happy. Goldie cuddled right into the squirrel's lovely fur, and it was just like a cosy rug.

"I'm so happy," she said sleepily. "This is better than squeezing in with the snakes—or getting a cold under the toad's stone—or hanging upside down with the bats! Good night, dear Squirrel! Sleep tight!"

They did—and on the first warm winter days they will wake, and you may see them hunting for the nuts that the squirrel so carefully hid away in October. If you see him, look out for Goldie—she is very much better at finding the nuts than he is!

THE
ASTONISHING BRUSH

ONCE upon a time Dame Lazybones went to do a little spring-cleaning at Wizard Twinkle's castle. She was just like her name, and never did a thing unless she had to.

Now, when she got to the castle Wizard Twinkle was just going out. "Good morning, Dame," he said. "Please scrub all the floors to-day—and do them well!"

He slammed the great door, and Dame Lazybones sighed and groaned. How dreadful to have to do so much work all at once! Then she spied something that made her chuckle with delight. The wizard had left out his magic book of spells.

The old dame ran to it and turned up "Scrubbing brush." She soon found what she wanted.

"To make a brush scrub by magic," she read, "take an ordinary brush, lay it down on its back, trip round it three times, cry, 'Romany-ree' as you go, and then kick the brush in the air, saying 'Scrub away, brush!'"

In great delight the old woman took the scrubbing-brush, laid it down on its back, and tripped round it three times, crying loudly "Romany-ree!" Then up into the air she kicked the brush, shouting "Scrub away, brush!"

The brush fell to the ground and then, to Dame Lazybones's great delight, it began to scrub the floor all by itself. You should have seen it! There was a large pail of soapy water just nearby, and the brush kept going to this and dipping itself in, and then scrubbing the floor with a fine, shishoo-shishoo-shishoo noise.

"Ah," said Dame Lazybones, sitting herself down in the wizard's own armchair with a pleased smile. "This is the best way to work—sitting down and watching something else!"

Well, it wasn't long before the old dame was fast asleep, and she snored gently whilst the scrubbing-brush went on working busily. It finished the floor of that room and went to the next. Then it went upstairs and did the bedroom floors. They were all of stone, and very dirty indeed, so the brush really did work hard.

At last all the floors were finished. The brush sat up on its end and looked round for something else to scrub. Ah yes! It would scrub the walls.

So it began. But it didn't like the pictures that hung here and there, so it sent those down with a crash to the floor. That woke up Dame

Lazybones, and she looked at the brush in horror.

"Stop! Stop!" she shouted. "What ever are you doing? Are you mad, brush?"

But the brush didn't stop. It began scrubbing the top of the stove and sent five sauce-pans, three kettles and a frying-pan flying off with great clangs and bangs.

75

Dame Lazybones rushed to the magic book and looked up the spell again—but to her great dismay there was nothing there about how to stop a magic brush from working. She didn't know what in the world to do. She rushed at the brush just as it was going into the larder, and tried to snatch it.

Crack! It gave her such a rap on the knuckles that she cried out with pain. She tried to get hold of it again, and once more it tapped her smartly on the hand. Then it popped into the larder and began to scrub the shelves, sending everything flying out into the kitchen.

"Oof!" said Dame Lazybones as a milk pudding landed on her shoulder. "Ow!" she cried as a jelly slipped down her neck. Crash! Smash! Down went dishes of jam-tarts, tins of cakes, joints of meat on the floor—and dear me, a large jug of milk crashed down near the surprised kitchen cat, who at once began to lick it up with joy.

"Stop! Stop!" cried Dame Lazybones, in horror, to the excited brush. But nothing would make it stop! It went next to the windows and began to scrub those, and down came all the curtains on the floor.

And just at that moment the door opened and in came Wizard Twinkle! Oh my, how Dame Lazybones shivered and shook.

"Oh, stop the brush, stop it!" she cried. But the wizard shook his head. "It has one more job to do!" he said—and as he spoke, the brush flew over to poor Dame Lazybones and began to scrub her too! Oh, what a way she was in! How she ran, how she fought that brush—but it wasn't a bit of good, it gave her a good drubbing, rubbing and scrubbing!

Then the wizard clapped his hands and said, "Romany-ree, Come to me!" The brush hopped over to him, stood by his foot and did nothing more.

"See what your laziness has done!" said the wizard, looking all round with a frown at the dreadful mess everywhere. "You will now clean up this place from top to bottom, Dame Lazybones—and never let me hear of your being LAZY again!"

"Oh, no, sir, no, sir!" wept Dame Lazybones as she hurried to pick up all the things lying on the floor. "Oh, I'll never be lazy again! Oh, that dreadful brush! Oh, deary, deary me!"

And you'll be glad to know that the old dame never *was* lazy again; she couldn't forget that astonishing brush!